The Noah's Ark

A big beautiful ark, with a sheep dog and a spotted dog, a black cat and a ginger cat, lions, tigers, caterpillars, crocodiles, and two of everything else, is given to George.

When George had gone to bed, taking Mr Noah to sleep under his pillow, the animals wanted to get out and explore. Mr Noah had the key of the ark in his pocket, and they were locked in; but the giraffes pushed with their noses, and the monkeys climbed up their long necks and got their hands into the crack. The roof slid along, and the animals, birds and insects flew and climbed out into the dark sitting-room. All except one wanted to play and explore. Mrs Hedgehog made a nest in a chrysanthemum pot, and in the morning there were six hedgehog babies.

In the excitement of their return to the ark next day George discovered the secret that though the animals and the Noah family felt wooden in George's hand, they were alive, and had been for a hundred years.

The Noah's Ark

Ruth Ainsworth

Beaver Books

First published in 1969 by
Lutterworth Press
Luke House, Farnham Road, Guildford, Surrey, England

This paperback edition published in 1976 by
The Hamlyn Publishing Group Limited
London · New York · Sydney · Toronto
Astronaut House, Feltham, Middlesex, England
© Copyright Text Ruth Ainsworth 1969
ISBN 0 600 36571 9

Printed in England by Cox and Wyman Limited, Reading
Set in Monotype Baskerville
Line drawings by Elsie Wrigley
Cover illustration by Christine Molan

Contents

Chapter One

George has a Surprise

'I don't know what to do,' said George.

'Why not paint?' said his mother.

George shook his head.

'Or have a tea-party?'

George shook his head again.

'Or dress up and I'll guess who you are?'

But George shook his head.

'It's raining too fast to do anything exciting,' said George, 'and I only want to play out of doors.'

As the rain was tumbling down and the windows were streaming, this was impossible, and George knew it.

'I know,' said his mother suddenly. 'I've something in the attic that I think you'll like. I played with it when I was a little girl and I'd forgotten all about it. I'll run up and get it.'

George stood at the bottom of the ladder that led to the roof. He could hear his mother moving boxes and making noises. He jumped up and down to make the time pass more quickly. Then, at last,

his mother appeared, with a big bundle in her arms, wrapped in a silk shawl. She came down the steps slowly, because she hadn't a hand to hold on with.

'Quick! Quick!' said George. 'I can't wait another minute.'

They went down to the sitting-room and mother undid the silk shawl. George sat back on his heels and just looked and looked.

'Oh Mother, a Noah's Ark. A beautiful, beautiful Noah's Ark, with a little window in the roof, and pointed windows round the sides, and a door at each end. I must see what's inside.'

The ark was like a big, wooden boat, with curling white and blue waves rippling round it. The waves were painted on. There was a house inside the boat with a red, sloping roof and a dove on it. The house held all the animals.

George soon found that the roof lifted off, and he began to take out the animals and birds, just as they came.

There were two of everything, though it was sometimes a long while before he found both of each pair.

'Two cats,' said George, 'a black one and a ginger one. Two monkeys, just the same. A ram with horns and a sheep with just wool on her head. A sheep dog and a spotted dog. And two, tiny, tortoises.'

'I used to put the tortoises last,' said his mother, 'when I set the animals out in a long procession. They crawled so slowly. I put the lions first because the lion is the king of beasts. The tigers were second because they looked royal with their stripes.'

'Who are these?' asked George, holding up two pretty little green and yellow birds.

'I called them colly birds because I never knew

their real name. And I called those birds over there the never-never birds, because they never never would stand up straight.'

George tried to stand them up, and they both fell over.

'I shall call them the never-never birds too,' he said.

There were ladybirds with spots, and stags with antlers, and crocodiles with flat, green tails. There was everything he could think of.

'There must have been lovely toy shops when you were a little girl,' he said.

'Oh, these never came from a toy shop,' said his mother. 'A clever man made them for your grand-mother. He finished off everything properly, the hoofs of the horses and the tails of the pigs and the tiny legs of the ladybirds.'

'It must have taken that clever man years and years and years,' said George. 'It must have taken him all his life.'

When George had taken everything out, he began to sort out the Noah's Ark people. It was easy to find Mr Noah as he had a long white beard and a crook in his hand. Mrs Noah wore a striped dress. The sons and their wives wore different colours. Mr and Mrs Ham wore blue. Mr and Mrs Shem wore green. Mr and Mrs Japhet wore red. Each man had a stick in his hand and a flat hat on his head. Each woman had a white apron and a handkerchief round her head, except Mrs Noah who had a hat like a flower pot.

'It's nearly bedtime,' said mother, 'and it has stopped raining. Do you want to run round the garden for a breath of air?'

George usually loved doing this, but he was hardly listening. He was examining the faces of the Noah's Ark people. Ham looked cross, though his wife was smiling. Mr Noah looked like a king. He *was* a king in a way. He was the head of everyone and everything in the ark.

'Do you want a run round the garden?' asked mother again. 'You could take one of Noah's Ark people or animals with you. They've been shut up for twenty years.'

'Yes, I will,' said George, springing up. 'I'll take Mr Noah with me. Will you hold him while I put my boots on?'

Mr Noah liked the dripping wet garden. It reminded him of the forty days and forty nights of rain, when the earth had been flooded and he and his family and the animals floated safely on top of the water in their ark.

George shook a drop of rain off a leaf on to Mr Noah's head to let him feel its wetness. His breath of air lasted so long that mother had to call him in to go to bed.

'May I have Mr Noah in my bath?'

'Yes, but be careful. We don't want his paint to wash off.'

George floated a toy boat he had in the bath, with Mr Noah for a passenger. He made little waves and the boat rocked up and down. Then he made bigger ones, and then such monster ones that Mr Noah was flung out. Fortunately he did not mind as he could swim, and George soon rescued him.

That night, Mr Noah, carefully dried on George's handkerchief, slept under George's pillow.

Chapter Two

Let's Explore

When George was asleep, and his father and mother had gone to bed, there was a great deal going on in the ark.

'I'll be head of the ark as Father is not here,' said Ham, frowning severely and frightening the smaller animals with his stern voice.

'We don't need a head for one night,' said Mrs Noah gently. 'Dear Father will be back with us tomorrow. We can surely live at peace till then.'

'How do you *know* he'll be back tomorrow?' said Ham. 'I don't trust that boy George. Perhaps he lost Father in the garden, or let him go down the plug hole with the bath water.'

Mrs Noah looked sad and worried, but was relieved when Japhet, her youngest son, spoke up.

'I trust George absolutely. His mother always took care of us when she was a child. George will be just the same. Remember how carefully he lifted us out, one by one.'

'And put us all the right way up,' said a colly bird.

'He admired my tail,' said the peacock, who was rather vain.

'He wasn't cross when I fell over as I always do,' said a never-never bird.

'He treated me with great respect,' said the lion. 'He knew I was the king of beasts.'

'Let's explore a little now we have the chance,' said Mrs Noah. 'I know Father would like us to stretch our legs. But how are we to get out as the key of the door is in Mr Noah's pocket?'

'We are clever,' said the monkeys. 'We have hands and we might be able to pick the lock.'

But though they fiddled and fiddled with the lock they could not undo it.

'You're not as clever as you think!' said Ham, who liked saying disagreeable things.

'We might be able to slide the roof along, or lift it somehow,' said Mrs Noah.

'Let the bigger animals come to us, at this end,' said the elephants. 'We can all heave together and slide the roof along. Then we can get through the opening.'

'Here we are,' said the hippopotamuses.

'Here we are,' said the rhinoceroses.

'Our long necks may be useful,' said the giraffes.

'And our humps,' said the camels.

'We'll come because we have hands,' said the monkeys.

'No one wants you,' said Ham. 'You are only little animals.'

'But we can grasp and pull and push,' said the monkeys, showing their little hairy hands, with quick, clever fingers.

'What are you two silly creatures doing, getting into everybody's way,' said Ham to the two tortoises.

'We are like stools,' said the tortoises. 'The others can stand on us to make themselves taller.'

'A very good idea,' said Mrs Noah, stooping to stroke their heads.

In the end the giraffes pushed with their noses and the monkeys climbed up their long necks and got their hands into the crack. The roof slid along and left an open space. Then there was a terrible scramble to get out, little animals standing on bigger ones, and Ham shouting:

'One at a time! Wait till I call your names!'

Of course nobody waited and before long the ark was empty. Mrs Noah was the last to get out as she helped the little ones like rabbits and moles. The climbing animals, like the squirrels, were out in a flash, almost as soon as the birds.

The sitting-room seemed full of birds. They perched on the pictures and the clock, and sipped water from the vase of flowers. A monkey switched on the light, which was comfortable for those animals who could not see in the dark.

Ham was still cross because no one had listened to his orders or obeyed him. He and his wife walked up and down on the polished table in a dignified way.

Everyone else was wild with excitement. The sheep dog rounded up the sheep and the goats and drove them into the coal scuttle. The monkeys swung from the lights. The tortoises warmed themselves by the fire, which was almost out. The cats joined them, and curled up on the hearth.

Most of the animals had almost forgotten what a room was like after twenty years inside the ark. The cushions on the sofa were like great pink mountains and the elephants toiled up them and then slid joyfully down. The camels joined them in this game.

Hide-and-seek was exciting in a place with so many good hiding places but there was trouble, as usual, with the snakes. They hid in impossibly difficult places, under the edge of the carpet, and down the cracks of the armchairs. There were cries of 'Not fair!' and 'You can't play!'

Then Mrs Noah clapped her hands and said: 'Time to go back home,' and though the animals had taken no notice of Ham and his shouts, they did what dear Mrs Noah told them at once. She was like their mother.

'I can't have a roll-call,' thought Mrs Noah, 'as the list of animals is in Mr Noah's pocket. But I expect we are all here. Why should anyone stay behind? And I see that the door into the hall was safely shut, so no one could get lost that way.'

What neither Mrs Noah nor anyone else knew was that someone was missing. Someone was not in her place in the ark when they settled down for the night.

Chapter Three

Mrs Hedgehog

Mrs Hedgehog did not go back to the ark with Mr Hedgehog and all the other animals. She had not intended to stay behind, or run away, but when Mrs Noah clapped her hands and said: 'Time to go home,' Mrs Hedgehog did not hear. Some people thought that the hedgehogs hadn't any ears because they were hidden under their prickles, but this was not true. They had ears like anyone else, and good ones, too. But Mrs Hedgehog was not in a suitable place for hearing.

Mrs Hedgehog had had a strange feeling for some time. She had a great wish to make a nest of something. Unfortunately there was nothing that would do in the ark, so she had to be content with dreaming that she was making a nest. Every night she made dozens of nests of leaves and moss and dried grass, and was quite low-spirited when she woke up and found they were not real.

On the wide window sill there was a large flower pot with a chrysanthemum growing in it. The flowers were shaggy and white, and the leaves were dark green. Mrs Hedgehog climbed up the side of the pot and found herself standing on moist brown soil, with the leaves all round her. They smelled strongly but not unpleasantly. One by one

she tore off the leaves that were low down, and she scratched and scrabbled till she made a hollow in the soil and lined it with the leaves. It was exactly as she had dreamed a nest to be, dark and secret and snug. When the monkeys turned the light off before they went into the ark, it was even darker and more secret. Mrs Hedgehog arranged herself comfortably, and before morning, when George's mother came in to draw back the curtains, she had given birth to six baby hedgehogs.

The hedgehog babies were dear little mites. Mrs Hedgehog loved them because she was their mother, but if anyone else could have seen them they would have loved them too. Their prickles were pale and soft, not in the least like their mother's hard stiff ones, and their eyes were tightly closed. In a few days they would open, and the babies would be able to see their mother's loving, prickly face bending over them. They gave little, high cries except when they were asleep, which was most of the time.

'I do wish Mr Hedgehog could see them,' said Mrs Hedgehog to herself. 'He does not know what remarkably fine children he has, two sons and four daughters. I wish Mr and Mrs Noah could see them as well. But I don't think Ham would approve. He is always saying the ark is too crowded and of course six more animals will make it worse. Especially as they are such healthy babies and will doubtless grow into large, strong hedgehogs.'

It was not long before Mrs Hedgehog got the fright of her life. She had just fed the babies and was settling down for a nap when Polly, George's cat, came into the room. She too intended to have a nap, curled up on the rug by the fire. But something stopped her. She uncurled herself and sat up straight. Her whiskers twitched and the tip of her tail beat the floor. She heard what only a cat's ears could have heard, some faint, high squeaks.

Polly was an experienced cat and knew at once that they were not a mouse's squeaks. They stopped almost at once, as the hedgehog babies dozed off, but Polly was too uneasy to settle to her nap. She sprang on to the sofa, and then on to the back of the sofa, and surveyed the whole room. There was nothing unusual to be seen. She jumped back on to the floor and began to prowl about in the hope that there would be something to smell. Under the table, under the chairs, round the skirting and behind the desk she went. Several times she visited the pot of chrysanthemums and sniffed delicately round it. But she could only smell the strong smell of the flowers and leaves.

She went back to the hearth rug and curled up and closed her eyes. Why should she have her afternoon nap spoilt by a squeak? Even if it *had* been a mouse, she had just eaten a large dinner of liver and could not manage another mouthful. Nor did she feel like a chase after something small and cunning that would bolt down a hole hardly big enough for a kitten's paw. All the same, just one more look at that plant pot would put her mind at rest. It seemed just an ordinary plant but one never knew.

She padded silently across the carpet, sniffed yet again, crouched low and sprang up upon the pot. She landed on something prickly and gave a loud, indignant mew.

'Whatever next!' said Polly crossly, licking her hurt paw. 'This is a respectable house, I'd have you know, and whoever you are you'd better go back to where you belong.'

'It's you who should apologise,' said Mrs Hedgehog, her prickles standing on end alarmingly. 'Here I am with my young family, doing no harm to anybody, and a large, green-eyed monster pounces on us. It is lucky that I am so well protected with my exceedingly sharp prickles. You, I notice, have only a few short prickles on your feet. A very bad arrangement, I must say.'

'I can tell you that many animals are afraid of my claws and of my sharp teeth,' said Polly. 'I am noted as a hunter. Few mice, rats or birds dare set foot in our garden.'

Mrs Hedgehog, though she had spoken bravely, was rather in awe of Polly herself. She decided, for her children's sake, that it would be better to have her as a friend than an enemy.

'Yes,' she said, 'I have heard of you and your exploits, and I must add that I have never heard that you have attacked any members of my family. Our paths seldom cross. I wonder if you would care to see my babies? You will be their very first visitor. They were born only last night.'

Polly gazed with wide green eyes at the hedgehog babies. She considered them very inferior to her own kittens, but she, too, preferred to have this prickly person as a friend, so she said:

'Very fine indeed. Very promising children. I see their eyes are not yet open. I can recommend frequent licking with the tongue. I have found this helpful with my own kittens.'

'Yes, I too believe in frequent washing,' said Mrs Hedgehog.

'I see there are six,' said Polly. 'I myself have never had more than five in a family.'

The two mothers forgot their differences, and a long, absorbing conversation took place, dealing with the care of babies, their upbringing and general management. When they had finished, each thought that there were many likenesses between baby hedgehogs and kittens. Polly's paw stopped hurting, and Mrs Hedgehog had stopped trembling.

'How did you come to choose this plant pot for your nursery?' asked Polly.

Then Mrs Hedgehog explained her great urge to make a nest and that this seemed the first suitable place. Polly was very sympathetic.

'I know that feeling so well,' she said. 'Before I have a family I get very restless and go round the house inspecting cupboards and drawers and beds. But whatever place I choose, George's mother always finds me and moves me to a box under the kitchen table. I find this very trying, though the kitchen is warm and the larder is next door. How long do you intend to stay in your present nursery?'

'I hardly know. I should like Mr Hedgehog to see the children as soon as possible. Perhaps I can join him when the babies are bigger.'

'I've no patience with fathers,' said Polly. 'Mr Tom never comes near me. He leaves me all the burden of training and care. He wouldn't know how to wash a kitten properly, much less feed it.'

'But these are my *first* children,' said Mrs Hedgehog. 'I feel sure that Mr Hedgehog will be extremely proud. And I know that Mr and Mrs Noah will be proud too.'

Polly shook her head unbelievingly.

'I'll tell you this,' she went on. 'You'll have to move by tonight.'

'But why?' said Mrs Hedgehog.

'Because every Friday morning the plant is watered and your children will be drowned.'

'Oh how awful!' cried Mrs Hedgehog. 'I've been saved from one flood in the ark, and now I'm threatened with another. What day is this, please?'

'Why, it's Thursday.'

'However do you know? You must be a well-educated cat.'

'I know because I have liver for dinner on a Thursday, and I had liver today.'

'Then there's only today. What do you advise me to do?'

'When next the ark is opened, you must slip back.'

'Yes indeed. That is what I must do. But carrying six such young hedgehogs will be no joke. I hope I shall have time to carry them back to safety.'

'Stop worrying,' said Polly. '*I* will help you. I notice that the children are not yet prickly – quite soft, in fact.' She touched one with a paw. 'I can carry two or three at a time. We may only need to make two journeys.'

Mrs Hedgehog had terrible visions of Polly

swallowing a child by mistake, but she decided to trust her.

'Thank you,' she said. 'You are very kind.'

'I will continue my nap here, on the window seat,' said Polly. 'No one will know I am here and I will come and help you at the right moment. Have no fear. I will not fail you.'

She disappeared behind the red curtain and Mrs Hedgehog lay awake, wondering if she had done the right thing. Polly was so large and her mouth was full of needle-sharp teeth. Well, she would hope for the best.

Chapter Four

The Rescue

George had been unable to play with his Noah's
Ark all day. He had had to go with his mother to
see his aunt. He took Mr Noah with him and they
had some nice games while the grown-up people
were talking. His aunt gave him some dominoes
to play with and he built a house for Mr Noah,
with a path for him to walk along, and a bridge
across a river for him to cross by. Mr Noah
tried to be happy, but he was worried about
Mrs Noah and the family, and all the creatures
in the ark. When would he get back to them, he
wondered?

George got home soon after tea, and tore off his
coat, and got the Noah's Ark out. He took off the
lid and began to take out the animals. He put Mr

Noah beside his wife and they were able to tell each other all the news.

'Are you all right, my dear?' asked Mr Noah.

'Yes,' said Mrs Noah.

'And are the children safe?'

'Yes.'

'And the birds?'

'Yes.'

'And the animals?'

Mrs Noah looked so distressed that Mr Noah put his arm round her.

'There were so many,' said Mrs Noah, 'and I hadn't the list to have a roll-call as it was in your pocket, and – and – well, one of them is missing.'

'Which one?'

'Mrs Hedgehog.'

'Then I'd better talk to Mr Hedgehog.'

One of the dogs ran off to find him and he soon arrived, his prickles drooping, and his eyes dull with weeping.

'She was the best wife a hedgehog ever had,' he said. 'Never a cross word. Always trying to please me.'

'Where did you see her last?'

'We got separated when Mrs Noah let us out of the ark for a midnight frolic. I myself climbed up the neck of one of the giraffes and got out that way, and I spent my time playing follow-my-leader with the moles. Then when I was safe back inside I looked everywhere for her. I searched every nook and cranny. The monkeys helped me, and the dogs. But she wasn't to be found anywhere.'

'We'll find her, we'll find her,' said Mr Noah. 'I'll call a general meeting and see if we can pick up a clue. Tell the others, please, Ham.'

This was the kind of errand that Ham enjoyed. He shouted and waved his stick and clapped his hands, and at last the animals were arranged neatly in rows, waiting for Mr Noah to begin.

'Now we must do all we can to get Mrs Hedgehog back,' said Mr Noah. 'Think very carefully. Did any of you see her last night when you were having your frolic? Please try hard to remember.'

'I saw her,' said a camel. 'She used my hump to stand on so she could scramble out of the ark. She was rather prickly and scratched me a little, but no one could take offence. She was so polite. She kept apologising for hurting me.'

'I saw her,' said a goat. 'She was heading for the window sill. I asked her if the leaves of the plant in the plant pot were good to eat. She said she thought not. Then we parted.'

'The next thing to do –' began Mr Noah, but he

never finished his sentence. Polly the cat landed beside the ark with a soft thud, and her mouth full of three hedgehog babies. She dropped them gently in the ark, murmured, 'I'm going back for more,' and disappeared.

A moment later she was back with two more, and Mrs Hedgehog arrived with the last one.

'There's no need to be scared,' said Mrs Hedgehog, seeing everyone huddled at the far end of the ark. 'Polly is as gentle as a lamb. She has brought my babies to safety for me. She hasn't harmed even a prickle. These are the first babies to be born in the ark, and without Polly they would all have been drowned!'

There was a murmur of: 'Drowned! How awful!'

Then Mrs Hedgehog told them about the nest under the chrysanthemum, and how the plant was watered every Friday. 'And tomorrow *is* Friday,' she said at the end. 'If we had stayed in the nest, streams of water would have come down upon us. I might have survived, but there would have been no hope for my babies, so young and tender and their eyes not open yet.'

'Oh dear!' sighed the more sympathetic of the animals.

In spite of Mrs Hedgehog's soothing words, the animals remained huddled as far away from Polly as possible. Then Mr Noah stepped forward, though his knees were shaking, and said in a quavery voice:

'We thank you, Mrs Polly, for your great kindness to one of our number. You have undoubtedly saved the lives of our youngest and most precious children. If we can ever do anything to help you, just ask.'

'Thank you,' purred Polly, her deep voice filling

the animals with fresh terror. Some of the more timid ones put their paws over their ears.

Polly strolled over to the hearth rug. The baby hedgehogs had left a queer taste in her mouth. A mouthful of prickles was so very different from a mouthful of soft fur. In the ark, Ham was scolding Mr and Mrs Hedgehog.

'As if we were not crowded enough,' he said crossly. 'We're for ever tripping over each other and finding it difficult to select a space big enough to sleep in. Now you have actually dared to add six hedgehogs to the company. Not one or two, but six! You are selfish and stupid. It might have been better if the children had been drowned. You would soon have forgotten about them.'

'We wouldn't!' said the Hedgehogs. 'Not ever!'

'Well, I would soon have forgotten about them. I must talk to Father. When the children are a little older they must be got rid of. Perhaps they could be lost in the garden. Wild hedgehogs are quite happy living outside.'

Just then Polly's head appeared over the side of the ark, her green eyes glaring and her tail lashing. She seized Ham in her teeth and shook him.

'If I ever hear you even suggesting that Mrs Hedgehog's children are a nuisance' – shake – 'or ought to have been drowned' – shake – 'or must be got rid of '– shake – 'I'll carry you to the top of the tallest tree I know and I'll leave you there. The crows will peck you and you'll never, never get down again. Do you understand?'

'Yes,' said Ham.

Polly gave him another shake, just to make sure, then dropped him, and returned to the hearth rug.

'You deserved that, my boy,' said Mr Noah. 'I never thought to hear a son of mine speak so unkindly.'

George watched this scene without stirring a finger, or saying a word. He watched Ham getting the animals into line, and heard Mr Noah talking to them, and then, most surprising of all, he saw Polly arrive with her mouth full of hedgehog babies. He had been frightened when Polly came back and shook Ham, though of course Ham deserved a shaking for being so unkind.

He was not sure how he felt about the discovery that the Noah's Ark people and animals were alive and could talk and feel. Would they mind him playing with them? He must ask someone about this. Perhaps tomorrow? Mr Noah would be the best person to ask. He put the animals back into the ark. They felt wooden in his hand, but he set them down gently. As he put on the lid he heard Mrs Noah singing a lullaby to her lapful of hedgehog babies.

Chapter Five

Mr Noah Explains

When George's bedtime came, he took Mr Noah upstairs with him and stood him on his bedside table. When he had had his bath, there was always a little time before his mother put out the light. He usually looked at a book then, but tonight he took Mr Noah and settled him in the bedclothes, facing him.

'Mr Noah,' began George. 'I never knew till today that you were alive and could talk.'

Mr Noah made no answer. He did not even blink an eye.

'Mr Noah,' began George again. 'Perhaps I've upset you by treating you as if you were – well, as if you were just a wooden person with no feelings. I won't ever do it again.'

Still Mr Noah made no answer. He never stirred. He really looked as if he were just as wooden as wooden could be.

'Please, please Mr Noah,' said George once more. 'Please say just one little word. I want to know we are friends. If I made you cross by playing with you and floating you in my bath and

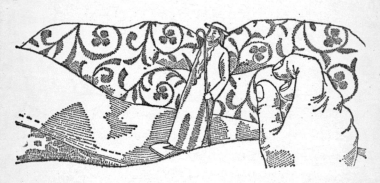

putting you under my pillow, then I'm very sorry. I simply didn't understand. I won't even play with you again if you say you don't like it. Really I won't. Or I'll try not to,' he added, wondering how he could keep away from the Noah's Ark and its wonderful contents.

'Noah's Arks are made to be played with,' said Mr Noah suddenly. 'It's what we are here for. The more we're played with the more we like it. We've been played with, off and on, for a hundred years. We had a long rest when your mother was grown up and you were not old enough to play with us, but now it's all right again. The day you took us all out of the ark, one by one, was a red-letter day. You should have heard the joyful chatter when you put us back. Cows mooing and sheep bleating and birds singing and lions roaring. It was like birthday and Christmas Day all rolled into one.'

'Shall *I* ever hear you making a joyful chatter?' asked George.

'I don't suppose so,' said Mr Noah cheerfully.

'But why not? Why ever not?' asked George.

'Because when you play with us we know how to behave. We are proper wooden Noah's Ark animals and people, who can't talk or move or do anything by themselves. Stand us up, and we stand. Lay us down, and we lie still. Move us here and there, and we go without a word. That's how we've always been, and that's how we shall always be. Just wooden.'

'But what will happen when I'm not there,' said George. 'When nobody's there, and you're all alone?'

'That's when we come alive,' said Mr Noah. 'I take charge, helped by my dear wife and my sons, and we walk about, or skip about, or run or creep as suits us best. We have adventures, and sometimes we quarrel. We play games, and make merry.'

'Don't you like the being alive times better than the being wooden ones?'

'We like both. We couldn't do without either. You see we were made to be wooden people and animals. That's our real life. The other times when we come alive make a nice change, that's all.'

'Do you mind that I saw you and heard you this afternoon, when Polly came along with the hedgehog babies in her mouth, and Ham was cross?'

'We were all so excited by Polly's visit, and by the birth of the hedgehogs, that we hardly noticed you were there,' said Mr Noah. 'They are the first babies to be born since the ark was built.'

'Did you mind Polly shaking Ham?'

'Not a bit! It will teach the boy a lesson. He mustn't be so keen on law and order. He's not a bad boy, really, and he does a great deal to help, making sleeping arrangements so that we all have enough room, and so on. Of course the six hedgehog babies will make us even more over-crowded than we are at present. But we shall make room somehow. Where there's a will there's a way.'

Just then George's mother came in, kissed him good-night, and switched off the light.

George put Mr Noah under the pillow and settled for sleep.

'Good-night Mr Noah,' he whispered.

But Mr Noah was his most wooden. He never said a word and stayed without moving till morning.

Chapter Six

The Colly Birds

The animals in the Noah's Ark knew that they had counterparts in the world, much, much bigger than they were themselves. The camels knew that large, humpy camels crossed the desert on long, swift legs. The tigers knew that immense tigers lived in the forest, slipping through the shadows and the bars of sunlight. The peacock knew that a bird like himself, with a flashing tail like a vast fan, stepped across green lawns, delighting all who saw him. Each animal knew that he had a double, though few had actually *seen* their double.

The cats, the black and the ginger, had taken some time to get over the shock of seeing Polly. They still had nightmares about her though she had done them no harm. Such teeth! Such claws!

Such a long, lashing tail! And such glowing green eyes! But they felt important, all the same, to be related to such a majestic animal.

You might wonder how the wooden, Noah's Ark animals got to know about their doubles. I will tell you how this came about.

The owl was a very wise bird, and he could read. He could not only read easy words like THE CAT IS ON THE MAT, he could read long difficult words, in very small, black print. The monkeys, who had hands, brought books from the bookcase and owl read aloud to anyone who wanted to hear. One of the favourite books was a very large one in ten volumes called: *THE NATURAL HISTORY OF THE WORLD*. This book had something in it about every animal in the ark, and there were pictures too. Lions and leopards and llamas, snakes and squirrels and sheep dogs, all were there.

Owl was very fond of reading about himself, which was natural, but he was willing to read about other people too, when asked. When a very timid animal, such as a mouse, asked to hear about mice from the big book, owl would turn the pages with a careful claw till he came to the right place, then he would start reading about field mice and house mice and harvest mice and long-tailed mice and many other kinds of mice. Once a mouse dared to ask:

'Please, sir, which kind of a mouse am I?'

'An ordinary mouse, my little fellow,' said owl, 'which is far the best kind to be.'

The colly birds were the only creatures who did not appear in any of the Ten Big Books. They begged owl to look a second time to make sure he had not missed them. He looked most carefully, but there was no mention of the colly birds.

'Perhaps two pages have got stuck together,' said one colly bird. But though owl scratched delicately with his claw, and blew through his beak, he could not find two pages stuck together.

'Perhaps there is a page missing,' said the other

colly bird. 'Look through the numbers in the corner of the pages and see if one has been left out.'

This took a very long time, but at the end owl reported that all the numbers were there.

The colly birds were very pretty, with green and white feathers. The monkeys, who were always teasing, called them Cauliflower Birds and asked them if they liked cheese sauce, which is often eaten with cauliflower. The colly birds held their heads high and did not reply, but their feelings were hurt just the same. They lay awake at night, wondering who they really were. Were there, somewhere in the world, real colly birds with green wings and snow-white ruffs under their chins? Surely there were. There must be.

The colly birds began to worry and to go off their food. They began to moult green and white feathers. Then one night, as they perched side by side, unable to get to sleep, Mr Colly said to his wife:

'It's no good worrying like this and wondering who we are. We must *do* something. We must go out into the world and see if we can find some live colly birds. Then we can tell all the other animals about them, and they will respect us. No one will dare to call us Cauliflower Birds again!'

'Or ask us if we like cheese sauce,' said Mrs Colly Bird. 'How shall we get out of the ark?'

'We can hide somewhere, like Mrs Hedgehog did, when we have our midnight frolic.'

'But remember that Mr Noah calls the roll. When we do not answer he will come and look for us.'

'Perhaps we should tell him and he will help us. He always helps anyone who is unhappy.'

'Yes, that would be best. We will tell him our troubles and he will let us go.'

The next morning the colly birds asked Mr Noah if they could go into the world and look for real live colly birds.

'Must you go?' said Mr Noah sadly. 'The world is big, and you are very small. The world is full of dangers, and the ark is safe and peaceful. And you are dear to me, and I cannot easily spare you.'

'But we *must* go,' said the colly birds. 'We are the only creatures not described in the Ten Big Books that owl reads to us. Surely, somewhere, there are birds such as we are, only bigger, stronger and more beautiful. We hope to find them.'

'Very well,' said Mr Noah sadly. 'I can see that your hearts are set on going. Please take great care, and come back safely to me.'

Mrs Noah gave them an extra feed of grain for breakfast, and when they could eat no more, Mr Noah opened the little window in the roof and the colly birds flew out, feeling very brave.

'Good-bye!' said all the other animals. 'Good-bye! Come back soon!'

The colly birds planned exactly what to do. They would hide behind the curtain till George's mother tidied the room, as she always opened the window so that she could shake the duster out of it, and the colly birds hoped to dart out before she shut it again.

Everything went as they had planned. George's mother laid the fire, and dusted the room, and shook the duster out of the window. She was so busy that she never noticed two little wooden birds, not much bigger than bees, who fluttered out into the garden. She shut the window with a bang and went off to the kitchen, singing to herself.

'I do hope they'll be all right,' said Mrs Noah. 'I don't feel at all comfortable. They are so small and inexperienced. I wish you hadn't let them go.'

'But they would have fretted,' said Mr Noah. 'Already their feathers were coming out and they were off their food. When they come back, their minds will be at rest.'

'When they come back!' repeated Mrs Noah.

'I'm afraid that won't be till Sunday follows Monday,' which was her way of saying they might never come back.

Chapter Seven

The Colly Birds Abroad

If it had been summer time, the colly birds would have met many friendly creatures in the garden. There would have been butterflies and bees, grasshoppers and caterpillars. But on this day there was no one about. There was frost on the blades of grass and on the fallen leaves.

'It's very quiet,' said Mr Colly Bird, hopping across the lawn.

'And very lonely,' said Mrs Colly Bird, hopping after him.

'We will ask the very first person we meet,' said Mr Colly Bird.

'If we ever meet anybody,' said Mrs Colly Bird.

Just then they came upon a worm who was pulling a dead leaf down into his burrow.

'A serpent!' whispered Mrs Colly Bird.

'Not at all, madam. I'm just an earth-worm,' said the worm. 'Can I do anything for you?'

'Oh yes please,' said Mr Colly Bird. 'Have you ever seen any other birds like us?'

'But much bigger, of course,' added Mrs Colly Bird.

'I can't say that I have,' said the worm. 'The white reminds me of a dove or a pigeon, and the green is a little like a linnet or a greenfinch. But the two together – no. I've never seen that. What are your names?'

'We are called the colly birds.'

'I wish I *had* seen some other colly birds,' said the worm. 'Your colour scheme is particularly attractive. But there's never been one in this garden. Can you sing?'

Mr Colly Bird immediately ran up and down the scale, and Mrs Colly Bird followed, a tone or two higher.

'No, I haven't heard that song either.'

'Thank you,' said the colly birds. 'You have been very kind.'

They hopped off together.

'We'll ask the very next person we meet,' said Mr Colly Bird.

'If there is a next!' said Mrs Colly Bird, whose feet were getting cold.

Soon after this a large, black crow swooped down out of the air, missing the colly birds by inches.

'He's dive bombing us,' said Mr Colly Bird. 'He'll get us next time. Quick, let us fly up into this tree and hide.'

They flew up on their tiny wings, and what with the cold, and being frightened, they never would have reached even the lowest bough, but Mr Colly Bird saw a hole in the trunk.

'Quick! In here, my love!' he gasped. They felt safe and sheltered in the hole, and they watched the black crow swooping down again and again, looking for them.

When their hearts had stopped thumping with fear they examined the hole more closely. There was a jumble of leaves and moss in one corner and a sound of deep breathing. Somebody was in bed.

The hole did not feel so safe now. Any moment the person might wake up and would certainly be annoyed to find two strangers in his bedroom.

'I don't think I could fly at the moment,' said Mrs Colly.

'I'm trembling all over. I've never been so frightened in my life.'

'What of?' said a sharp little voice from the corner, and out came a brown, furry face, with bright eyes, and pointed, tufty ears.

'Of the crow. It swooped down on us from the sky. I saw its beak and its claws. Horrible! Horrible!' said Mrs Colly Bird.

'Nasty things, crows. Well, you're quite safe here. I don't suppose you know who I am?'

'Oh but we do. Indeed we do. You are a squirrel.'

'Yes, that's my name. Where have you met any other members of my family?'

'In the Noah's Ark. We are very friendly with them. Please, please think very carefully before you answer this question. Have you ever seen any other birds like us?'

The squirrel stared, and his wife woke up,

rubbed her eyes, and stared too. Then they both shook their heads.

'No, never. You must be very uncommon.'

'But we don't want to be uncommon,' said Mrs Colly Bird sadly. 'We should like to have other birds like us. Then people would write about us in books, and draw pictures of us. No one shows us any respect, as it is. They don't take us seriously.'

'I think you are beautiful,' said Mrs Squirrel. 'Such a soft shade of green, and the white ruffs are so becoming. But you are so very – so very delicate and petite, that you will be safer back in the ark. The world is full of perils. We could tell you a sad story of owls that have robbed our own nursery and made off with our babies.' She sighed, and wiped her eyes.

'Please go back to the ark,' begged Mr Squirrel. 'What my wife says is quite true. The world is full of perils.'

'We don't want to give up yet,' said Mr Colly Bird. 'We want to make quite sure that there are no other colly birds about. Supposing there is only one more – even that would be better than nothing. We shall search on a little longer.'

'And supposing – supposing you search in vain?' said Mr Squirrel.

'Then we shall go sadly back to the ark and give

up all idea of being important, and having our names and our pictures put in books.'

'You must do what you think best,' said Mrs Squirrel, 'but please, please be careful. A crow, or even a starling, would swallow you in one beakful. And on the ground there are dogs and rats and stoats with sharp teeth, who would snap you up in a twinkling.'

'We will be very very careful,' said the colly birds, and after thanking the squirrels for their kind advice, they left the hole in the tree and fluttered slowly towards the ground on their tiny wings.

They hopped down the path which was more sheltered than the lawn, and then round to the side of the house. Soon they found themselves near the wire netting of the hen-run.

Seeing the large, strong hens strutting about, scratching and cackling, their first impulse was to hide. They crouched together under a fallen leaf, where they could see and hear what went on without being seen. They soon discovered that the wire netting was intended to keep the hens in, and the spaces in the wire were too small for even a hen's head to poke out. They could hear the cock, a very fine gentleman with a red comb, talking in a bossy voice.

'Out of my way at once. I need a drink. Stand back there. What's that you've found, a slug? Remember I have first peck of anything tempting.'

A very motherly speckled hen was scratching just the other side of the netting. She was saying, 'Ch – ch – ch!' to herself as she scratched with her clean yellow feet.

'Let's ask her,' said Mr Colly Bird. 'I don't feel frightened though she is so big.' He cleared his throat and said loudly:

'Excuse me, Mrs Hen – '

The hen looked all round to see where the voice was coming from.

'Here we are,' said Mrs Colly Bird. 'We're just the other side of the netting, under this dead leaf.'

The hen peered through the netting and presently she saw them.

'Bless me, what charming little birds. You remind me of a newly hatched chick, except for your colour. I'm afraid you're very cold. Won't you pop through one of these holes and I'll spread my wings over you? I'm never so happy as when I have something small warming under my wing.'

'It's very kind of you, very kind indeed, but what we really want is information. Have you ever seen a colly bird like us, but of course much larger?'

The hen looked at them with her head on one side.

'Never,' she said, when she had had a long look. 'Never in a hen-run and never in the garden. You must be very rare. I feel it is an honour to have met you.' She gave a low bow.

'But we don't want to be rare! We want to be ordinary, with other birds like us.'

'It's better to be rare,' said the hen. 'Look at our fine cock. There's only one of him, and dozens of us poor hens. He gets treated like a king, with the first peck at anything good, and the best place in the hen-house to perch in.'

But the colly birds couldn't be comforted.

They said good-bye to the motherly hen and

fluttered towards the house, tired out by their adventures.

'Let's wait in the porch,' said Mr Colly Bird. 'Someone is sure to open the door soon, and then we can slip in.'

They waited side by side on the mat, and when George's mother came home from shopping and turned her key in the lock, they flew inside. They tapped on the little window of the ark and Mr Noah let them in.

'My dear, dear children,' he said. 'I feared some harm had come to you. But here you are, safe and sound.'

Chapter Eight

The Extra Page

While the colly birds were out in the world, looking for other birds just like themselves, George
was playing with his Noah's Ark. He was arrang-
ing the animals in groups, according to their
colour, with one of the Noah's Ark people to
take care of each group. Ham was in charge of
the spotted ones, the giraffes and leopards and
ladybirds. Shem had the striped ones, tigers
and zebras and caterpillars. Japhet had the plain
brown, lions and camels and bears. Their wives
were given the odd ones, like the black and white
badgers and the black and white cows. Mr and
Mrs Noah had the birds who were too spotted,
striped, ringed and blotched to fit into any group.

Although, of course, the Noah's Ark animals

and people were being wooden and silent, George felt they were not as wooden and silent as usual. He put Mr and Mrs Noah several inches apart with the birds round them, but when he next looked at them he saw they were close together, with their heads nearly touching. They were whispering, he was sure.

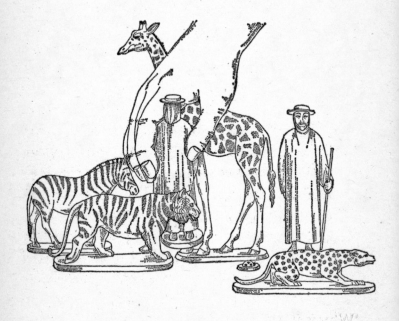

The birds were especially restless, fluttering their wings when he wasn't watching, and hopping here and there. When George went to look out of the window he heard a murmur as if everyone were whispering and shuffling and rustling.

'Mr Noah,' said George, 'what is wrong? Why are you all fidgetting and talking behind my back?'

At once everybody froze into their most wooden. Not a foot or a feather stirred. Not a head turned. Mr Noah not only looked wooden, he looked stupid as well.

'Mr Noah,' begged George, 'do remember that I know your secret. I know you are really alive. Don't bother about my knowing, but just tell me what is the matter. I can tell you're not happy. Why, I might even be able to help you.'

'Shall I tell him?' said Mr Noah to the animals.

'Yes,' sighed a hundred voices. 'Yes! Yes! Yes!'

'Very well,' said Mr Noah. 'Now you may not have noticed, but two of our family are missing.'

'Who?' said George.

'The colly birds!' said everyone together.

'Oh, you mean those dear little green and white birds? I'm very fond of them; I'd never heard of them before. They must be very rare.'

'That's the trouble,' said Mr Noah.

'Why is it a trouble?'

'I will explain. Monkeys, please run and fetch me *The Natural History of the World*.'

The monkeys ran to the bookcase and came

back with two volumes. Then they ran back for two more, and two more, till all ten volumes were on the table.

'We are all in these books,' said Mr Noah importantly. 'Elephants and eagles, camels and crocodiles, the whole lot. But the colly birds are missing.'

'Are you absolutely sure?' said George, who could not read himself and wondered if Mr Noah could.

'Absolutely sure. Owl can read and he has looked through the books, page by page – '

'Page by page,' said owl.

'And read them line by line – '

'Line by line,' said owl.

'And even word by word – '

'Word by word,' agreed owl.

'And there's nothing about colly birds. The colly birds are very upset by this, and they have gone into the world to see if they can find any live colly birds, or even hear news of any. They are small and timid, and we fear they may come to some harm. That's why we haven't been as wooden as usual. We are all anxious.'

'Worried to death!' said Mrs Noah.

'We fear the worst!' said Ham.

'We may never see them again!' said Shem.

'If only they would have stayed in the ark with us!' said Japhet.

'It's partly our fault because we teased them and called them the Cauliflower Birds,' said the monkeys.

'I think they'll be all right,' said George. 'They are very small and can hide easily. And they can fly. It's a very frosty day and I think they'll be back soon to have their feet rubbed. But we have work to do. We mustn't waste any more time standing around.'

'What can we do?' asked several voices.

'If there's no page in all those great books about the colly birds, we must write one and stick it in somewhere. Nothing else will satisfy them and make them feel important. It would be better to type one. Can anyone type?'

'We can,' said the monkeys. 'We often type for fun when we are having our midnight frolic. But we can't spell.'

'I can spell,' said owl. 'I can read *and* spell. But I don't know what to spell.'

'I can make up the words,' said George, 'though I can't write them down. Let's put some paper in the typewriter and we'll begin.'

The monkeys took the lid off the typewriter and put in a clean sheet of paper.

'Has anyone noticed any special habits that the colly birds have?' asked George.

'I once saw them drinking dew from a spray of honeysuckle,' said a canary.

'In the spring, Mr Colly Bird collects grass and Mrs Colly Bird collects moss,' said Mrs Noah. 'Now that we are safe on land once more I think they may build a nest.'

'Anything else?'

'They don't like the cold,' said a duck. 'They try to perch in the middle of the ark, away from the draughts.'

George thought for a few minutes, and then began to speak, not too quickly, as owl had to spell every word to the monkeys before they could type it.

First George said a few words. Then owl spelt them aloud. Then the monkeys typed them. It took a very long time, but luckily they had the whole morning to themselves. George's mother was making the Christmas cake in the kitchen, and there were no disturbances. This is what was on the extra page:

COLLY BIRDS. – Colly birds have green and white feathers. They have a sweet song which goes up and down. They live in sheltered places and drink the dew from the flowers. They make their nests of grass and line them with moss. They are rare, and anyone who sees a colly bird is very lucky indeed.

The page of typing looked important when finished. George drew a picture of a colly bird at the bottom and coloured the green parts with green crayon. Then he got some paste from the desk and stuck the page at the very end of Volume 10.

'When the colly birds come back we'll show them the page, as if we had just found it,' said George. 'Owl, you can read it to them. Perhaps you'd better run through it now to make sure you can manage all the difficult words.'

Owl put on his most serious expression, cleared his throat, and read it without a mistake.

'Well done! Most impressive! They'll be so proud!' commented various animals.

The books were put back on the shelf, the paste in the desk, and everyone was safely back in the ark when there was a tap-tap on the window in the roof. Mr Noah hurried to open it, and the colly birds fluttered down on to his hand.

'My dear, dear children,' said Mr Noah, 'I

feared some harm had come to you. But here you are, safe and sound.'

'Have you found what you wanted?' asked Mrs Noah.

The colly birds shook their heads sadly. 'No, no,' they said. 'We consulted a worm, a pair of clever squirrels and a wise mother hen, but none of them had even heard of a colly bird.'

They looked very disappointed and hid their faces in their white feather ruffs.

'Cheer up,' said Mr Noah. 'While you were away *we* have made a wonderful discovery. Monkeys, please fetch me Volume 10.'

The monkeys scrambled away and soon brought it to the table. They turned the pages till they came to the very end.

'Look!' said Mr Noah. 'An extra page that we missed before. An extra page all about you!'

'About us!' gasped the colly birds.

'Yes, about you. Owl, please read the page aloud. Not too fast, so the colly birds can take in every word.'

Owl put on his reading face, cleared his throat, and began.

When he had finished, Mr Colly Bird said:

'Please could you read it once more?'

Owl obliged.

Then Mrs Colly Bird said:

'Please could you read it just once more, for me?'

Owl obliged again.

'No more now,' said Mr Noah firmly. 'We must wait for our midnight frolic. Then perhaps owl will read it yet again.'

The book was put back, and everyone returned to the ark. The colly birds sat together in a dream of happiness.

'White and green plumage,' whispered Mr Colly Bird.

'A sweet song,' whispered Mrs Colly Bird.

'Drink dew from flowers – '

'Nests of grass – '

'Lined with moss – '

'Very rare – '

'Anyone who sees us – '

'Is very very lucky indeed!'

They went on repeating the magic words till they fell asleep.

Chapter Nine

Another Flood

The rain fell for a whole week. Every day was wet, and every day George had to put on his mackintosh and his Wellingtons to go out. The garden was a sea of mud. Little rivers ran down the path from the front door, and out on to the pavement where they joined the dark brown river in the gutter.

At last the sun shone again and the drops of water on the twigs sparkled. The garden was still muddy, but George longed to go out and play.

'May I go into the field?' he asked his mother.

'Yes,' said his mother, 'but don't get any water over the tops of your Wellingtons. It may be deep after all this rain.'

'I won't, really and truly I won't,' said George.

The field was just at the bottom of the garden, and George could get into it through a little swing gate. The field belonged to Farmer Bodkin, but he never minded George playing there. There was plenty of room to play with a ball, or to fly a kite, and best of all there was a stream running through it.

It was a very small stream, and sometimes in summer it dried up altogether. But most of the year it rippled along with a line of reeds and tall grasses to mark its course.

Today, as George ran over the squelchy grass, he saw that the stream had grown into a small river. The line of reeds were showing only their tips. The light, rippling sound which the water usually made had changed into a low growl. Bits of wood were swept along with tufts of straw, and a scum of dead leaves.

George got as near to the stream as he dared, taking care that the water was not deep enough to go over the tops of his boots. He threw a twig in, and saw it whirled out of sight in a second. Presently a branch floated by, and this branch gave him an idea. Why not bring out the Noah's Ark and let it float in the flood water? Mr Noah was a good sailor, as he had once sailed his ark for forty days and forty nights, and come to no harm.

All the same, George thought it better not to tell his mother what he was going to do. She just might say no, and that would be a pity. He would call her to see the ark when it was floating.

George darted in at the front door while his mother was upstairs. He picked up the ark in his arms, and went back to the field. He found the big ark awkward to get through the swing gate and he had to hold it high above his head.

As he went squelch, over the grass he wondered where would be the best place to launch it. At one point there was a dip in the field and the flood water had filled it and made a pool. This would do well. The pool was calm and the ark could float there as if in a harbour. He waded a little way in and then lowered the ark carefully on to the water. It wobbled a little, and then righted itself, and sailed steadily.

'What a treat for Mr Noah and his children and all the animals,' thought George, who wished he were small enough to be inside the ark with them. They would be crowding to the windows to look out upon the watery world. Perhaps some of the smaller animals might be frightened, especially Mrs Hedgehog and the baby hedgehogs. So he shouted:

'Don't be afraid! This isn't a real flood. It's just

the stream over-flowing its banks. I'll bring you safely back to dry land in time for dinner.'

Though the pool *looked* calm, the ark was gradually sailing further and further from the place where George was standing. Soon it would be caught in the brown, swirling stream. He looked for a long branch with which to hook it back, but there was nothing suitable near by. He

waded out till the water got into one of his boots, but he could not nearly reach. So he stood where he was, one boot full of water, and watched his precious ark getting nearer and nearer to the stream. Directly it reached the rough water it swirled completely round twice, then sailed away with the tufts of hay and the dead leaves.

George ran along beside the stream. He could only run slowly because of the boggy ground and his waterlogged boot. He knew that the stream went on till it reached a wood. He was not sure what happened after that. He had never been so far. It might be best to run home for help. Giving a last look at his ark, George turned and ran home, stopping only once to tip the water out of his boot.

'Mother!' he gasped. 'Mother! Mother!'

He had run so fast that he had hardly enough breath to speak. He just gasped: 'Mother! Mother! Mother!' again and again. Gradually he got out a few more words – stream – flood – ark, and Mother understood. She washed the flour off her hands, and took off her apron and looked serious.

'I'll get out the car,' she said. 'We'll drive as quickly as we can to the bridge. The stream joins the river about there. Bring your fishing net.'

George grabbed his fishing net from the hall and they tumbled into the car, and drove to the bridge. They walked along the bank till they found the place where the stream joined the river.

'Has the ark raced us and gone away down the river?' said George.

'Oh, I don't think so. We came a quick way. The stream curves and bends and goes a long way round. I think we're too soon. We'll have to wait.'

So they waited. George held his net ready. It

was fixed to a bamboo handle and he would catch the end of the ark in the net, and bring it to the bank. He imagined it so often that he almost felt he had done it, and that the ark was safe.

Time passed. George's foot that had got wet felt cold and uncomfortable. A paper bag swept by, and more sticks. There was a sharp shower of rain but they did not leave their place. The bus went over the bridge.

'It won't come now,' said George.

'No, it won't,' said his mother. 'We must go home and have dinner. But don't be too unhappy. We'll get the ark back somehow.'

'Let's count twenty slowly.'

They counted very very slowly, but in the end they had to say 'twenty'.

'We'll go out afterwards and go all along the bank of the stream,' said his mother. 'We shall find the ark somewhere, stuck in the mud – '

'Or caught on a stone,' said George.

'Or safe on the bank.'

Neither of them said what they were both thinking, which was: 'Or sunk to the bottom, with all the people and animals drowned!'

Chapter Ten

Lost, a Red Noah's Ark

George had a little rest while his mother washed up. He usually took Mr Noah to have a rest with him, or one of the animals. His hand felt empty with nothing small to hold. Then they both put on boots and their oldest coats, and went to the field. They decided to follow the stream, if they could, right to the bridge where it joined the river. They followed it across Farmer Bodkin's field, and over another field, and through the little wood. This was difficult as the ground was muddy and there was no proper path.

They had to push their way through bushes, dipping under branches, and once climbing over a fallen tree. It had fallen right across the stream with all its branches on, and some dead brown leaves. It was difficult to scramble over as there was nowhere to put their feet, and the branches got in the way and stung their faces.

Always they watched the stream. Surely they would soon see something red, caught in the undergrowth or stranded on a mud bank. But they saw nothing red, except a red packet that had once contained a breakfast cereal.

After the wood was another field where some black and white cows were feeding.

'Moo! Moo!' said the cows, huddling together under an oak tree. 'Moo! Moo!'

'Do cows eat things that aren't grass?' asked George. 'Would they like to chew something made of wood?'

'They only eat green things and vegetables,' said his mother.

So George stopped thinking about Mr Noah being swallowed by a hungry cow.

Soon they came to the river.

'Where can my ark possibly be? Where can it have gone?'

'I just don't know,' said his mother. 'We'll pin a notice on the gate to say it is lost. Perhaps someone may find it.'

'But who would be out for a walk on such a soaking day?'

'Well, you and I are out for a walk. And I suppose the farmer visits his cows to make sure they are safe.'

They put a notice on the gate, and mother rang up Farmer Bodkin to see if he or one of his men had found a Noah's Ark.

But the answer was no.

George's father said he would go and look at the week-end. It was no good going out in the dark.

'But we've looked!' said George.

'Then I shall look again. I shall take a stick and poke about in the bushes. I shall look very, very carefully.'

'*We* looked very very carefully,' said George. 'Mother and me.'

In spite of the notice on the gate, George felt he would never see his Noah's Ark again. The notice said:

LOST – A RED NOAH'S ARK
Will anyone finding it please return
it to this house. There will be a
reward.

'What will the reward be?' said George.

'Fifty pence.'

'My Noah's Ark is worth five pounds. No, it isn't worth money at all, it's far too precious. The clever man who made it would never have time to make another. Is he still alive?'

'No, he can't be. It was made a hundred years ago.'

The evening was very long, though his mother read to him. The evenings would always be long now. There were so many different games he used to play with his Noah's Ark. Mr Noah had become a real friend.

George could not cheer up, not even when his father played 'bears' with him. He usually laughed all the while he was being chased, but not this time. Not ever again. He knew that his mother minded almost as much as he did because she had spent hours and hours playing with the ark when she was a little girl. Mr Noah was her friend too.

Chapter Eleven

Captain Noah

When the ark was first launched on the water, Mr Noah was delighted. 'We're afloat! We're afloat!' he called out, and everyone crowded to the windows to look out. Mr and Mrs Hedgehog lifted up their babies so that they could see the water all around.

Mrs Noah and the other ladies were not pleased, and neither were the smaller animals, but when George shouted that they were quite safe, and would be back for dinner, they stopped being frightened.

Ham, Shem and Japhet stood beside their father and looked out at the flood. The ark rocked up and down and they felt like real sailors. Suddenly the ark swung round twice, and began to sail quickly away down the stream.

'Drop the anchor!' cried Mr Noah, but the anchor could not be found. Since they had gone to live on dry land no one had bothered about it. 'Drop the anchor!' cried Mr Noah again, but there was no way of stopping the ark as it hurtled along.

Mr Noah, with Ham, Shem and Japhet, stood

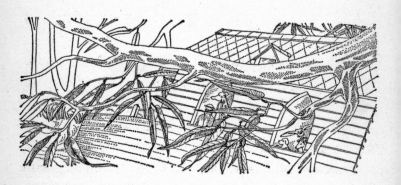

at the end of the ark on the pointed platform. 'Catch hold of any branch you can reach,' said Mr Noah. But the ark was going so fast that even when they clutched a willow, it was torn out of their hands. They could not hold on.

'Shall we be carried into the river?' said Mrs Noah.

'Leave everything to me,' said Mr Noah calmly.

'And then we may be carried down the river into the sea?'

'If that happens, I shall sail the ark towards

land. Remember, we once sailed safely for forty days and forty nights.'

'But who will save us?' said Mrs Noah, wringing her hands. 'We are so small, and the sea is so big.'

'A passing ship,' said Mr Noah.

'Or an aeroplane,' said Ham.

'Or a helicopter,' said Shem.

'Or George's father in a motor boat,' said Japhet.

'But what shall we eat?' went on Mrs Noah. 'We stocked up with food before our forty days on the water.'

'We shall catch fish,' said Mr Noah. 'The sea is full of fish. The three boys can fish for us.'

'And we will fish too,' said the monkeys, who had clever hands.

'I hope fish will agree with our babies,' said Mrs Hedgehog to her husband. 'It is not what they are used to.'

The colly birds seemed quite undisturbed. Ever since they had been shown the extra page in Volume 10 about colly birds they had been blissfully happy.

'We might see other colly birds flying over the sea,' said Mr Colly Bird. 'The book did not *say* we were sea birds, but I myself feel quite at home on the water.'

'So do I,' said Mrs Colly Bird. 'I like the motion and am not in the least sea-sick.'

Just then there was a dreadful crash as the ark collided with the fallen tree. It tilted alarmingly and became tightly wedged among the branches. One side was against the muddy bank.

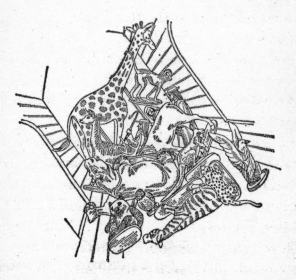

Mr Noah and his sons were swept off the platform, but they succeeded in climbing back again, scrambling from branch to branch.

The jolt had tumbled the animals into a heap, the smaller ones squashed by the bigger ones. They disentangled themselves, rubbing their bumps and bruises. The baby hedgehogs were almost suffocated, and had to be patted on the back. Ham, as usual, was ready to sort out any muddles.

'Stand in pairs!' he ordered, 'so we can see if you are all there.'

One ladybird was missing but was found buried in the wool of one of the sheep.

Mr Noah looked out of every window in turn, even the little one in the roof.

'The water is so high,' he said, 'that there is not room for the ark to float under the fallen tree. We are wrecked in its branches.'

'Are we safe?' said the hedgehogs, always thinking of their babies.

'We are safe for the moment,' said Mr Noah. 'If the stream rises higher than the window sills, we shall have to abandon ship, and try to get home overland. We are not many miles off and the dogs will find the way.'

'Bow-wow! So we will!' barked the dogs.

'Leave the ark!' said several horrified voices.

'Better leave it than drown,' said the tiger, who didn't care for the idea of swimming.

'We will post a watch,' said Mr Noah, 'to keep an eye on the rising water. The boys can take it in turns. Ham, will you take the first watch?'

'Yes, Father,' said Ham, taking up his position

at one of the windows where he could see the level of the stream.

'Shem can relieve his brother in an hour, and then Japhet can relieve Shem.'

Everyone settled down. Ruffled feathers were smoothed, and rumpled fur put in order.

'We are safe for some hours yet,' said Mr Noah. 'Perhaps even till morning. I myself shall have a little nap. The day has been rather too exciting. I advise you all to have a rest too.'

The cats had already curled up, and the hedgehogs rolled up, and some of the birds had put their heads under their wings, when the roof of the ark was lifted and an immense whiskery face peered in. The creature had sharp white teeth, rather pointed.

'Whatever have we here?' he said. 'Something most peculiar!'

Chapter Twelve

Toys for the Children

'Who are you?' said Mr Noah, starting up from his nap.

'I am Water Rat,' said the brown, furry, whiskery person. 'Who are you?'

'I am Mr Noah, and with me are my wife and family, and all my animals. This is my ark. You have just removed the roof without asking my permission.'

The Water Rat inspected them for some minutes in silence. Then he lifted up Shem in his mouth. Shem struggled and screamed and he put him down. Then he lifted up a lion – an ostrich – an elephant, all of whom behaved like Shem, and had to be put down.

'You're a fussy lot in this ark,' said Water Rat

rather crossly. 'You behave as though I'd bitten you, or swallowed you, or something. But you are curious and rather fascinating creatures. I shall take you down my hole to amuse my children. They are bored because I can't allow them out in

this terrible weather. They are very young and might be swept away. They've been squabbling and fighting all day. But I'm sure they'd love to play with you. The more you screamed and kicked the more amused they would be. It would keep them happy for hours. I'll take these funny little prickly creatures,' and he grabbed two baby hedgehogs.

Now among the Noah's Ark animals were two land rats. They were not special favourites, and rather kept themselves to themselves. But at this point Mr Rat emerged as a hero. He stepped forward and said in his loudest voice:

'I am a Land Rat as you are a Water Rat, so we are cousins, I am pleased to meet you.'

This was not absolutely true, as Mr Rat's knees were shaking with fright.

'Well I never!' said Water Rat dropping the two little hedgehogs. 'I never knew I had any cousins. I'm pleased to meet you, Cousin Rat.'

'As we are so closely related,' went on Land Rat, 'you can't treat me, or my friends – ' he pointed to the other animals – 'as toys for your children. It wouldn't be right. It wouldn't be cousinly. We are certainly no toys to be thrown about, and perhaps damaged. We have feelings just as you have.'

'I suppose not.' Water Rat was bitterly disappointed. 'It was such a good idea, and would have kept the youngsters happy for ages. I wonder if any of you would – er – would volunteer to be toys for an hour or two?'

There was silence. No one was going to

volunteer to be bitten, scuffled, tossed, and perhaps torn to pieces by the young water rats.

Then Mr Noah stepped forward. 'If your children like stories, I will offer myself as a story teller. I have had many amazing experiences in my life. Building the ark and floating in it for forty days and forty nights was an exciting adventure. And now being ship-wrecked in a tree.'

'That's very kind of you,' said Water Rat, brightening up considerably. 'They are very fond of stories and have heard all mine at least twenty times. Please let me conduct you to my house and you can start right away. Listen, I think I hear the children fighting again. My poor wife will be quite distracted.'

Sure enough, from the depths of a hole in the bank came the sound of scuffling and squealing. The animals shuddered as they listened.

'Keep a good watch, my sons,' said Mr Noah, and he followed Water Rat into the hole.

'Yes, Father,' said the three sons. 'We will.'

Almost at once the scufflings and squeakings stopped, and there was silence. Mr Noah had begun to tell the story of how he built the ark.

Ham stayed by the window, watching the level of the water. Land Rat was exhausted. He was being shaken by the paw, and patted on the back, by all the surrounding animals.

'You have saved our lives!' they said. 'Brave rat! Noble rat! Hero of the ark!'

Gradually the animals settled down once more for a nap. Only Ham kept watch. The water was still some way below the window sill, but it might rise. Then they would have to abandon the ark. Ham imagined himself lining them up in rows, and holding a roll-call. Everything should be done correctly, and in an orderly way. He would keep a specially sharp eye on the monkeys who were always playing tricks and upsetting the others.

An hour passed and Shem took Ham's place at the window. The stream rushed by, brown and growling, making such a din that Shem never heard the voices of George and his mother as they climbed over the fallen tree. Dead leaves caught in the branches almost covered the red roof of the ark. George and his mother never noticed it, half buried underneath.

Chapter Thirteen

One Good Turn

When Mr Noah reappeared at the mouth of the Water Rat's hole, it was plain that his story-telling had been a success. Water Rat shook his hand warmly and said:

'Thank you for a wonderful afternoon. You could have heard a pin drop, the children were so interested. Now I should like to do *you* a good turn, as one good turn deserves another. I should like to rescue you and your ark.'

'Rescue us!' said Mr Noah, 'but how?'

'I thought I would call five or six of my friends together, and between us we will push the ark up-stream till you are back in the field where you started.'

'Up-stream? But no one could swim against the current. It's impossible.'

'Impossible to you,' said Water Rat, 'and perhaps to all your animals, but not impossible to water rats. We are strong swimmers. I could not do it alone, but with help it could be managed. Would you like to be saved?'

'Of course. I should like it very much,' said Mr Noah.

'Then it shall be done.'

Water Rat whistled, and presently half a dozen fine, strong water rats came out of their holes, up and down the bank. Water Rat explained what he wanted done, and his friends agreed at once. They arranged themselves three each side of the ark, and the odd one pushed at the back. They soon freed the ark from its thicket of branches, and then began the journey back. It was not speedy as the journey down had been, but slowly and surely, inch by inch, the water rats forced their way upstream, holding on to the ark with their teeth and front paws, and kicking strongly with their back legs. At last they were out of the wood, and the crossing of the next field was less difficult. When they reached the field at the bottom of George's garden, they hauled the ark on to a piece of high ground near the swing gate.

Once more, Mr Noah and all his large family were on dry land.

The water rats were puffing and panting after their great effort, and rested for a time before starting back to their home.

'We shall hardly need to swim, the stream will carry us along as it carried you. Good-bye! Glad to have been a little help to you all.'

'Good-bye, and thank you,' called Mr Noah, and the animals waved from the windows. The monkeys climbed out on to the roof and waved from there.

'Let us all rejoice,' said Mr Noah. 'This is the second time we have come safely through the dangers of flood.'

Then Ham read the roll, and everyone answered when his name was called. Mr Noah locked the doors, and Mrs Noah went round saying goodnight, and giving the hedgehog babies a cuddle.

Chapter Fourteen

Home at Last

The next morning, George didn't go out to play. He wandered about the house, touching things, and thinking of all the games he could play with his Noah's Ark, if it were there to play with. His mother found him sitting half-way upstairs, tying knots in a piece of string.

'Why don't you go out now the sun is shining?' she asked.

'I don't know,' said George.

'Go into the field and see if the water is going down.'

'I don't want to see.'

'Well, I want to know, so could you go just to please me?'

'All right,' said George, slowly putting on his boots.

He stamped down the garden, plop, plop, in every puddle, and he felt more cheerful when he got to the swing gate. As he went through the gate, he remembered how he had had to hold the ark high up when he was carrying it.

The field was shining in the sun. The big pool had gone down so that he could see bits of long grass sticking up above the water. Then, quite near the gate, he saw the ark, its roof bright red, and the blue waves curling round it.

'Oh my ark!' cried George, running towards it. 'My beautiful, beautiful ark! Wherever have you been? How silly I was to let you be swept away.'

He picked it up and ran indoors, shouting:

'My ark has come home all by itself. Clever Mr Noah must have saved it somehow.'

His mother had no idea how it *could* have come home, and neither had George. When his father came home and heard the good news, he hadn't any idea either. The only strange thing was that there were dozens of tiny marks round the edge, almost like teeth marks.

George took every single animal and person out of the ark, and stood them on the table. They were all well and undamaged. Every one of the hedge-hog babies was safe. The never-never birds fell over and had to be propped up, but then they never, never could stand properly.

'Tell me where you've been,' said George to Mr Noah.

But Mr Noah looked his most wooden. He wouldn't even tell when he was in bed with George, held tightly in George's hand. Once George thought he put his finger to his lips.

'Well, keep your secret if you want, dear old Noah,' said George. 'I won't ask again.'

But though he did not ask again, he never stopped wondering.

More Beaver Books

We hope you have enjoyed this Beaver Book. Here are some of the other titles:

Through the Fire   The exciting story of how two Quaker children rescue their father from Bridewell gaol during the Great Fire of London in 1666, by Hester Burton

The Tail of the Trinosaur   Charles Causley's splendidly funny verse story about a prehistoric beast which comes to England from the Amazon jungle, with illustrations by Jill Gardiner

Snail Tale   A charming story about a snail and his friend, an ant, who go off on a journey

Midnight Adventure   The exciting story of how Tim and Gerry catch more than they bargain for when they go fishing at midnight; written and illustrated by Raymond Briggs

Read Me a Story   A collection of stories and verse for the youngest children, for reading aloud or for the children to read for themselves, edited by Frank Waters

New Beavers are published every month and if you would like the *Beaver Bulletin* – which gives all the details – please send a stamped addressed envelope to:

Beaver Bulletin
The Hamlyn Group
Astronaut House
Feltham
Middlesex TW14 9AR

365719